This book belongs to

_____

_____

_____

Going to school

It's recess time

It's noon

Going back home

Watching television

Story time with mom

Off to bed

MONTHS OF THE YEAR
January
It's winter again!

March

Spring is here at last.

April
Flowers have bloomed.

July
Bastille Day in France

August
Eating and eating

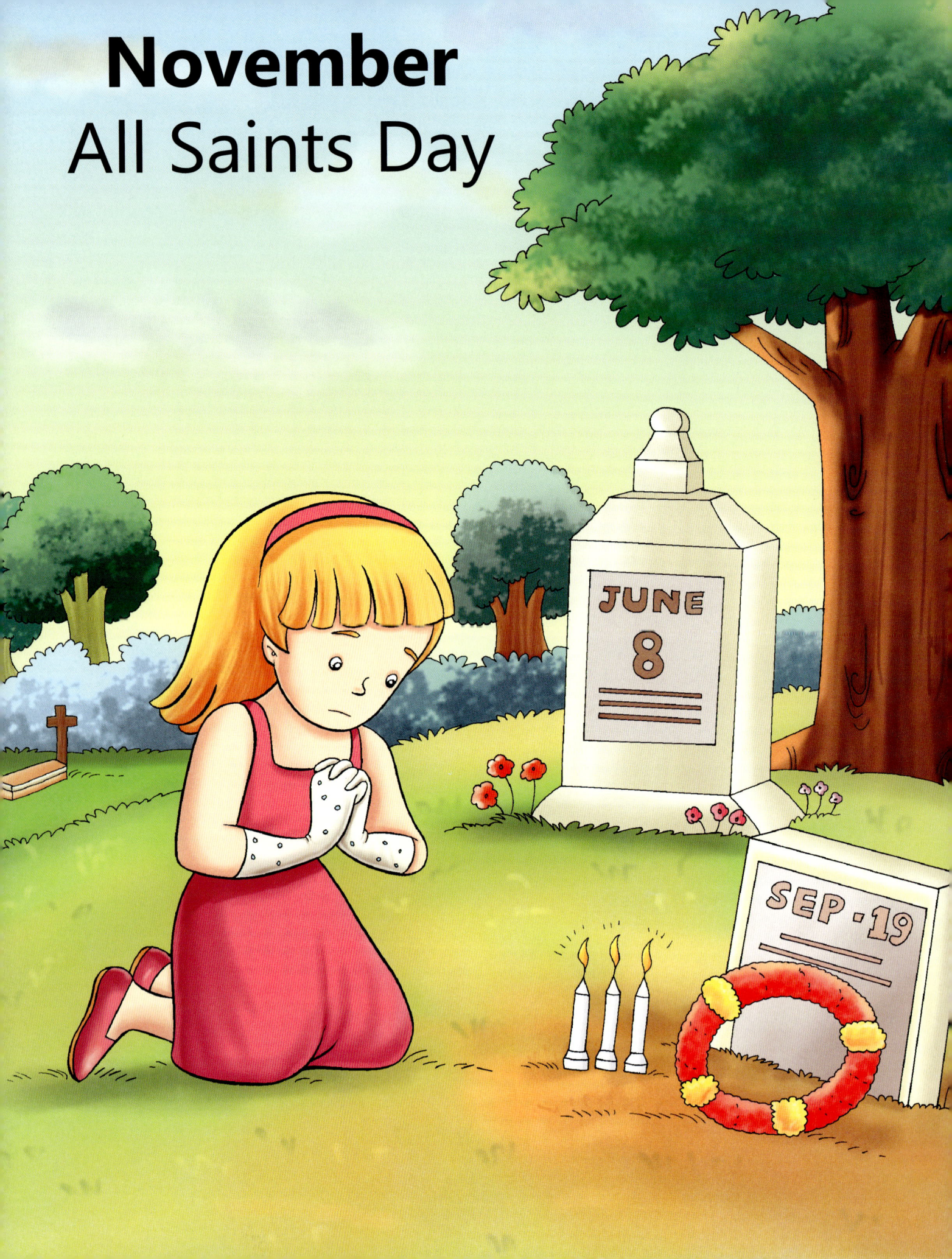

DAYS OF THE WEEK
Monday's child has an innocent face

Tuesday's child is full of grace

Wednesday's child is full of woe

And the child who is born on a Sunday is bonny, carefree, good and gay.